**Cemetery
of the
Lost**

2

Cemetery
of the
Lost

Barbara Neveau

Published by:
Barbara Neveau
P.O. Box 32
Essexville, MI 48732

Copyright © 2002 by Barbara Neveau
First Edition

All rights reserved. No part of this book shall be reproduced, stored in a retrieval system, or transmitted by any means without written permission from the author.

Cover design by Patti McTaggart

Printed in the United States of America
by: InstantPublisher.com

International Standard Book Number: 1-59196-087-8

Thanks to my family
and friends for their support and
encouragement during my learning
years. Without them, I would not have
had the courage to write and publish,
"Cemetery of the Lost."

A special thank you to
Mary Charbonneau,
the dedicated fact finder and
record transcriber for our
Bay County Genealogy Society. Mary
is the gal that planted the seed that
grew into the story of Mina, and she
never even knew
until now.

The poem,

Ten Thousand Thousand Bones,

copyright ©1995 by Mark Andrew Turcotte,

reprinted from *The Feathered Heart*

(Michigan State University Press, 1998, revised)

by Mark Turcotte,

appears by permission of the author.

Ten Thousand Thousand Bones

From long away, from
behind museum doors, from
darkly dusty rooms,

I hear Grandmother
rattling, she rattles,
among ten thousand thousand bones,
I hear Grandmother
rattling, she rattles.

She is frightened, alone,
among ten thousand thousand bones,
taken from warm belly Earth,
hot heart of Earth,
that was her resting home,

crying, cold
shaking on the shelf, alone,
    rattling,
among ten thousand thousand bones.

■   ■   ■

We wait for you Grandmother,
here in the wood,
where you belong.

The deer are stamping circles,
scratching at the ground,
leaning their ears
to listen for your song,
but you are gone.

The branches of the trees
all ache for you,
with their roots below
that once cradled you,
bending, reaching
to hear your song,
but you are gone.

The river moans
your missing voice,
the grass and stone
are silent
as they mourn
and listen listen.

The wings of hawks
call out your name and
    wonder wonder
where you've gone,

answered only by your rattling,
from where you shiver, cold,
alone,
among ten thousand thousand bones.

    ■   ■   ■

Grandmother, do not forgive
them, they know
what they have done,

taken you from
sacred circle light
and left you
in their tomb,
among all those other bones.

Fools,
they refuse to hear
the anguish in the Earth,
the cry of fox and rabbit
in your home.

Fools,
they refuse to fear
the angry step of Spirit Horse,
whose hoof
shall make a rattling
in their own living bones.

.   .   .

We wait for you Grandmother,
here in the wood,
where it's been so long.

The deer are scratching circles,
stamping at the ground,
leaning their ears
to listen for your song.

The branches of the trees
all ache for you,
with their roots below
that once cradled you,
reaching, bending
to hear your song.

The river moans
your missing voice,
the grass and stone
are silent
as they mourn
and listen listen.

The wings of hawks
call out your name and
   wonder wonder
where you've gone,
answered only by your rattling,
from where you shiver, cold
alone,
among ten thousand thousand bones.

Grandmother, do not forgive
them, they know
what they have done.

Acknowledgement

Many thanks to Mark Turcotte,
for permitting me to preface my book with his
gut wrenching poem,
Ten Thousand Thousand Bones
from his collection
The Feathered Heart.

12

Chapter One

While living in Florida with my husband and nineteen-year-old daughter, I had fulfilled my lifelong dream of becoming a writer. I now write articles and short stories for a number of New York magazines. Nora Kern Foster is my name, and freelance writing is not only my occupation, but also my obsession.

I prefer working, on my own, not in an office fending off nosy co-worker's questions. Of late everybody seemed to think my home life was open for discussion. Ever since they found out that the "Perfect Couple" had gotten a divorce.

Well, they would just have to live without answers to their rude prying. This gal wasn't hanging out our dirty laundry for others speculation.

That first year in college for our daughter Jamie had magnified the problems Jim and I was having. The isolation I began to feel.

The distance I knew was growing between Jim and I was compounded by the sameness in our routines. Wake up, shower and dress; grab a cup of coffee, give each other a peck on the cheek and dash off to work.

Jim never took me in his arms and kissed me the way he used to.

I knew the marriage had ended. Shriveled up on the vine from lack of the life giving elixir of love.

Jim, my ex-husband, my handsome lover of years gone by had become a graying, boyish, friend with whom I lived and shared a home. I was no longer willing to settle for that. There just had to be more.

When I asked for the divorce, Jim had been shocked. How could he not know that our marriage had dwindled to a boring pretense of passion?

"Don't you love me anymore?" He had asked.

I remember letting my eyes wander over him, seeing a six-foot tall stranger. His athletic build and the gray that streaked his auburn hair gave him a mature, successful demeanor. And that smile! I have always loved the crooked way he smiles. I hadn't seen it in a long time.

The first time I saw him smile my heart felt as though it had jumped into my throat. A friend had introduced us and when I heard his name was Stephen Foster, I burst out laughing.

"Yeah, that's your name alright and I'm Betsy Ross." I retorted.

" 'It really is my name, although I prefer to go by Jim Foster, it saves a lot of explaining. My parents wanted to give me an important name to insure my success in life. I have taken a lot of ribbing over the name, but that's all right too.' "

When he smiled again my heart had stood still. But that's another story, and I need to tell you about this adventure.

Looking around this place I now call home I felt the walls moving in on me. I longed for the spacious home Jim, Jamie, and I had shared for the last twenty years. I had been oh, so willing to give the house in Florida to Jim and keep the cottage in Michigan for my home.

Filling my days with wandering through shops, restaurants and, rummage sales in the surrounding small towns, I began hearing rumors of a little-old white woman.

Folks said she was strange and they rarely ever saw her anymore. No one knows why, but she tends the graves in a long forgotten Indian cemetery.

In the back of my mind was the thought that, if the tale was at all interesting, I might decide to write a short story for publication.

There were a lot of rumors passed down through the generations, but so far no one knew if they were really true.

Thinking that burying myself in work would push away the hurt and feelings of abandonment. I launched into this gem of a story with all the enthusiasm of an energetic bull terrier.

Sunday after church I dug out my work clothes, some pads to make notes on and a pair of sturdy shoes for trekking through the woods. Getting everything ready for tomorrow and what I considered a little one-day excursion.

The next morning turned out to be a warm, windy day, perfect for a jaunt in the woods.

Pulling on blue jeans and sensible shoes, and tying back my ash blond hair with a pretty piece of blue ribbon left by my daughter on her last visit, I went searching for this ancient graveyard and a legend.

It felt wonderful to be getting out of that stuffy cabin and away from the memories that filled every nook and cranny.

I spoke with some of the town inhabitants and found out that the caretaker lived in an old wooden shack near the cemetery, but didn't welcome strangers.

In an out-of–the–way area of northern Michigan, I found a desolate patch of ground with just a few markers left to establish the resting place of some long-ago inhabitants.

While standing there looking at this forlorn piece of ground with its peeling white wooden crosses, a small, wiry little woman with gray streaking her dull red hair came hurrying down the path to where I stood.

She wore a faded, flowery dress over gray slacks that barely reached her shoes. On her feet were ratty, old work shoes, scuffed from many years of use. Trendles of her hair had fought their way loose from the bun that tried to secure them, giving her the look of a mad woman.

From her stance, when she came to a halt, I had the feeling that she was ready for war. Although she only came up to my shoulder, I felt as though she could climb my five foot, eight inch frame and clean my clock, if she so desired.

I worked up enough courage to ask in a respectful voice, "Ms. Mallory, could you help me to discover the history of this graveyard and the names of the people buried here. Some of these people must have family that would want to locate their graves. If you would help me to record their resting-place, it would be a great service to the descendents?"

"Thought ya was some of those smarty aleck younguns from town, what with yer bein' in pants an' all.

"They git the idea ever once in a while ta come out and see what mischief they kin git inta. Shoulda knowed better cause they never come alone? Nobody ever comes alone, till now.

"Cain't tell ya' any history but kin tell ya' ' bout my life with the people. Ya kin call me Mina."

Now that she had decided that I presented no immediate danger, she relaxed and slowly began to relate the events leading up to the here and now.

Mina Mallory Youngblood is her name, caring for this old cemetery is her occupation.

She has been tending to the graves in this God-forsaken little patch of earth for over sixty years with the love and tenderness given only by someone who is dedicated to a dream.

She had a story to tell and I was willing to not only listen, but also record it for posterity.

Mina hadn't always been the strange little old lady that weeds the cemetery and talks to people unseen.

She vaguely remembers the happy times living at home with her mother, Pap as she called her father, little Mona, her younger sister, and Moses, her older brother. "I know you remember the life as sweet then, but would you go back?" I asked.

"No. My life was here with Henry and his people. I am part of the tribe now and here is where I belong, caring for the people and keeping the tribe alive to the world."

Mina agreed to tell me her story but only on her terms. I would be permitted to visit on Tuesdays and Thursdays; the rest of the time is hers to spend with her loved ones. These facts that follow, I only found out later after Mina and I had become friends.

Her world begins every morning at sunrise; arising from the single bed shoved far into the corner of the room. She starts the fire in the pot-bellied stove setting in the middle of the kitchen. The shack is built of wood and a piece of metal is nailed to the wall behind the pipe to prevent the heat of the stovepipe from igniting the wall.

She draws a small pail of water from the pump that stands on her cupboard, pumping vigorously until it is full. Fills a pot with water and puts it on the blazing stove to boil for her morning tea. While the water is heating she baths her hands and face in a blue, chipped enamel washbasin that brings back memories of another time.

She sheds the flannel nightgown that is too large for the feisty little lady and dons the work slacks and dress in accordance with the rules of the tribe.

"The women of the tribe do not wear pants alone!" She informed me.

This was a ritual she had performed for over sixty years. When her tea is steeped she takes it and a crust of stale bread and wanders out into the crisp cool morning air. She stands near an old oil drum, using it to hold her cup and stares off into the past.

"I was helpin'my pa git some vittles at the general store and the sunshine called me out onta the stoop. That was when I first laid eyes on him."

She smiles as she remembers the day she first saw Henry Youngblood.

"Dear God, he was beautiful, all bronze and shinnin', standin' tall in his buckskin leggings, chest smooth and tan, starin' off inta the deepenin' shadows of the woods. When he turned and our eyes met, my heart jumped in my breast, skipped a beat and then went lickity split to make up for the lost beat I guess. 'Twas the beginnin' of an affair that lasted a lifetime.

"Pap came out of Mr. Schmidt's General Store, took one look and jerked me back into that dark emporium filled with the pungent odors of pickles, rawhide, tanned skins, corn hangin' in bunches from the ceilin' and sawdust on the wooden floor. Now Pap didn't mind injuns much, but I 'spect he didn't want me foolin' round with one. Well, ya can imagine how I felt, comin' outa the golden sunlight of Henry, inta that black hole all stinky and such.

"Pap was jist a bit cranky bout my starin' at Henry, n said 'git yerself together girl. Cain't have ya standin' gawkin' like the town idiot, actin like ya ain't never seen an injun before.'

"Mr. Schmidt had ta put his two cents in with his opinion of those lazy, no account, drunken injuns. Him and his cronies should talk; they were always raisin' hell at Tom Russell's den of iniquity!

"Heard Pap say so lotsa times! Pap didn't hold with strong drink, but he didn't condemn them that does imbibe if they could hold their liquor and didn't make a fool of theyselves.

" 'Who is that young buck? Does he live round here?' Pap asked Mr. Schmidt.

" 'Sure does. Lives out in the woods beyond the pond at Fredrick Hand's place. The whole tribe is squatters on that parcel of land. Don't know who owns it, but there's gonna be hell to pay when they find out they are housing a bunch of dirty injuns on their land.'

"Pap, how can people say the injuns are dirty when that buck was the cleanest, shinniest man I ever saw? I asked.

" 'Girl, you don't know anythin' bout the world, so be shut! You speak when yer spoken to and not before.' Was all he said but it kept me still fer the time bein.'

"Well now, you don't know how willful I kin be when I set my mind ta it I decided right then I was gonna find out a lot more bout injun people, and this one in particular."

She chuckled at some secret memory that flashed through her mind and I knew there were some memories that I would never hear about, but could only guess from her reaction that Henry was a major part of those episodes.

Mina sat on a pile of neatly stacked logs under a giant oak tree at the edge of her yard.

An axe with a broken handle was imbedded in a chunk of wood along side of a weathered stump she used as a chopping block. I could hear tiny little scratching noises coming from the woodpile, but she didn't seem to notice. Her mind was back in another time.

Her shrunken frame looked fragile, but the fierce look in her large gray eyes told me of the inner strength that had stood her well through these long hard years.

She had to be in her eighties, but she walked tall and proud as a young girl when she headed to the silent place in the woods where her love and his family rested.

"They tell me stories of their life" Mina continued, "afore the white faces came cutting the trees and fencin' the land. How the ghost of the slain trees haunted their nights cryin' out ta them in dreams. The shame the whole tribe felt when they were banned from the General Store for stealin'. Chief Red Bird, who was in his nineties, went into the hills and died from the shame. The winds blew hard for three moons, mournin' his loss. The shock when they were told the land was no longer free; the white faces had put the land in jail behind fences and signposts."

A tear slid down the leathery cheek and dropped to the faded dress she wore.

How did you happen to get this job caring for this small cemetery? I asked.

"Ain't no job, least they don't pay me. If I don't keep it up they will plough it an plant corn, course it ud be the best damn corn they ever et. Let's see, when I first started weedin' here it was jist to be near Henry; I started droppin' by after work and then I started comin' on weekends.

"The truth is I jist want ta make my family's restin' place clean and comfortable. Pretty soon it was takin' all my free time, but I was happy because the other folks started talkin' ta me too. Henry told them I was ok, a part of him, so they came out too, when I come ta weed. That Henry, always waitin like I ain't got nothing else ta do."

Her face softened, eyes shone at just the mention of Henry's name.

This was a beauty that Jim and I had never shared. I wondered if I kept her talking if she would reveal the secret. I didn't know how to broach the subject of her and Henry, but she seemed to sense my curiosity, and asked me if I had heard the story of Henry Youngblood.

Thank you Lord! I now have an opening to some of the questions I wanted to ask.

"No," I answered, " but I would like to hear the whole story from you."

She shyly looked at me and I could see the impish look buried deep in her eyes, a small grin creased the wrinkled, elfin face, and she began a story so beautiful it just had to be recorded. It was a tale of love, hate, life, death, birth, and most important of all, devotion.

Her narrative was spread over many weeks. Every Tuesday and Thursday I would head out to her shack before sunrise and wait by the woodpile for her to open the door and greet the day. I tried bringing a thermos of coffee for her, along with my own, but she shook her head and steadfastly continued to brew her tea. I brought doughnuts fresh from the bakery, but again, shaking her head, stayed with her slice of dry stale bread.

The fieldmouse, she always fed a scrap of bread, had a feast when she crumbled a fried cake on the oil drum where he was sitting.

She walked as she talked and when we reached the place where Henry was buried she bent her head and mumbled something.

"Stay behind me an be quiet till I tell ya. The people are very shy and they don't trust strangers, cain't blame um now can ya?"

In her normal voice she announced, "I've brought a friend to visit with ya. She wants ta know the true story 'bout growin' up in this town and the special things in yer life. If ya don't want ta tell her yerself, ya can tell me and I will tell her." She listened for a few moments and so did I. All I heard was the wind rustling in the trees. Evidently she heard more.

"They don't trust ya, gonna have ta hear my tale first."

That was exactly what I wanted; her story was the one with all the mystery behind it. How did a white woman become the caretaker of an Indian graveyard and why did she remain steadfast in her task for over sixty years?

"Well now," she started, "ya all ready know how I first spotted Henry and how Pap felt bout that, but what ya don't know is that Henry felt the same way when he saw me. Ya could say that we was meant to be together forever. He followed us home so he could find out where we lived. He later told me he was tempted ta jist ride in and snatch me up and ride away like they did in the old days, but he wasn't sure how I would feel bout that and his horse was too old ta run hard.

"He hung round out in the woods for days, stayin' back far 'nough so's not ta be seen. Somehow I sensed him near and caught sight of him movin' from tree ta tree. I pretended not ta see him and would watch him outta the corner of my eye."

She sank down beside a sunken grave with a painted white wooden cross marking the place where Henry was buried and patted the earth.

"Now, now, dear one, I won't tell all, but we do want others ta understand a joinin'· that goes beyond all worldly things. I will tell her bout my peepin' out the window and watchin' ya climb that tree in the woods behind the barn. What do ya mean I got no shame? Ya were my man from the first time I set eyes on ya and I find no shame in that."

Her eyes sparkled with glee; she looked almost young again as she talked with her Henry. I now know what the unknown author meant when he said the eyes are the windows to the soul. Watching this touching scene, my mind conjured up images of warm summer nights by a campfire, sparkling brooks and in the distant memory were the drums beating a slow hypnotic rhythm.

Mina brought me back from my reverie with her teasing questions for Henry.

Her banter with Henry reminded me of the first few years of my life with Jim.

Those were wonderful years. I missed the togetherness during the day and his gentleness at night. His touch had sent shivers through my whole being. Where did it all go? Why didn't we feel it slipping away? Again the playful voice of Mina broke my reverie.

"Kin I tell her bout our first tryst? No? Why not? We was perfectly innocent of any unseemly behavior, course I cain't say that fer the second time. Was that a meetin'!

"Come on over here where he cain't hear. He's such a prude!"

I walked to another place where the earth had sunken and another white painted cross-marked the grave. "Who is in this grave?" I asked. "There is no name on the cross."

"Don't need names. I knowd where everbody is, sides I tried puttin' names on an' the sun an the wind wipes em away."

But Mina, others will want to know where these people are buried.

"Then they kin come an ask me!"

She closed the subject with a wave of her hand and knelt to touch the sunken patch of earth.

"This here's Henry's mother, Morning Star. She knowed bout our meetin' and was afeared fer us. She was a fine looking women, straight an trim as a arrow with a gray braid that hung down her back, an gentle brown eyes that glowed whenever she set eyes Gray Wolf.

"Gray Wolf, Henry's father, is here," indicating another sunken patch of earth next to Morning Star. "He was a handsome man too, straight an strong, course he weren't as handsome as my Henry.

"Gray Wolf didn't hold with our joinin', but then he was set in the old ways. He jist washed his hands of the whole matter. Gray Wolf was very brave but he did fear what my father would do when he found out bout me an Henry."

She bowed her head, tilted it slightly and peered up at me from mischievous eyes and whispered, "That Henry was some lover, damn near drove me wild!" She giggled shyly, "Ain't had nothin' since."

Her weeding done for the day she pushed herself up from the damp ground and headed in the direction of the shack she called home. I followed meekly behind; when we got to the oil barrel we parted ways, she into her shack and me walking the long path to my car. I was curious about Mina's abode, but considered myself lucky she was even talking to me. I believed those rumors that she wasn't always hospitable to strangers.

My notes were growing into a book and it took me hours to get back in the writing mood after I got home. Since I worked at home, Jim had allowed me to keep the two household pets, Snooks, an Alaskan malamute and Poodle mix, and Molly, a Jack Russell Terrier. The dogs needed to be let out and fed, the mail needed sorting and I was always behind in the household chores. I caught myself thinking how lucky Mina was; she wasn't tied down to this busy hectic world. Her world is tranquil.

The mystery of Mina was driving me crazy. She had some family in the area but she was alone in her solitude. Was it by choice or was there another reason why her family did not admit she was kin? The rumors were that she had gone injun and had turned her back on her family. They said her brother Moses had married a girl from the next town and had settled on the farm helping their ailing father.

When the younger sister, Mona turned sixteen she had taken a job as a domestic for some rich folks in Boston and was never seen or heard from again.

The towns' folk really had some wild stories about that choice little bit of information. One of the ladies swore she had seen Mona in New York and she was going by the name of Doris Downy and, heaven forbid, she was an actress!

That was many years ago and the story was never confirmed or denied, but it did grow with each telling.

That's another story that I may feel the urge to investigate someday.

"When Pap died, I went ta the funeral but stayed in the background, standin' near that huge old Oak that stood near the entrance of the graveyard.

"Ma saw me standing there during the prayer and made as if ta come ta me, but Moses grabbed her arm and pulled her back ta the open grave."

From the way folks talked about the scene at the funeral they were too busy watching what was happening with Mina and her family to properly pray for the newly departed.

She didn't tell me any of this. It was just the gossip that went back and forth through this deeply religious community over the years, and I expect each one added his or her own conception of what really happened. I can just imagine what the wake was like, all the busy bodies gathered together in one house. I never told Mina anything about the many versions I'd heard, but I'm sure she knew from the look I would see in her eyes before she put up the barricade.

"After watchin' Henry fer a couplea days, sneakin' round out back, I made my move. I hid out behind that great oak tree on Pap's farm and waited fer Henry ta come peepin' fer me. Ya shoulda saw his face when I jumped out an' surprised him! I still git a chuckle when I remember that look.

"Hush now, Henry, I ain't gonna spill the beans bout everthin', jist the whole story of us.

"The people have good ears; they hear everthin', cain't git away with nothin', she whispered. Anyway, we finally met an I thought I would choke ta death on my heart. It set in my throat the whole time we talked. Henry was jist as purty up close as he was from afar. I wanted ta touch his smooth tan face with my fingers but kept my hands ta myself till I knowed him better."

Her face shimmered with a glow that rivaled the sun; I could see the young girl that still lived deep inside the wrinkled old frame of Mina Mallory.

I questioned myself as to whether my love would have been as true and lasting as Mina's. If only all love and devotion could survive like Mina's, wouldn't life be a whole lot simpler?

Chapter Two

One chilly Tuesday morning I was there by the oil drum as usual, watching the field mouse making circles in the falling leaves, he seemed to sense that something was missing. He disappeared for a short time, and then was back scurrying around in the dry leaves as though trying to get me to follow. I went to Mina's door and knocked softly, but there was no answer. I knocked a little harder and heard what I thought was the wind in the trees moaning low. I listened with my ear against the door and the moaning was coming from inside the shack.

Pushing open the door I found Mina stretched out on the sagging old sofa, her face as white as the sheet that covered her.

"My God, Mina, what is it? Are you all right, can I get a doctor?"

"Ya come back tomarra and I'll be fine. Morning Star was here this mornin' and give me some tea made with roots, says it'll put hair on my chest.

"Who in hell wants hair on her chest?" She cackled.

Perspiration bathed her wrinkled old face, softening, and giving a silky sheen to her flesh. The fever enhanced her features, giving her face a childlike expression.

"Don't need nothin' now, got the magic tea in me, I'll be fine by mornin'."

"Please Mina, let me take you to the hospital, or at least let me bring old Doc. Prout. He can give you something to take down that fever."

I wanted to stay with her but she got so upset when I suggested it that I decided it would be better to leave and come back early in the morning. I glanced around her home and saw boxes of every size and description setting on every available table, chair, and cupboard. They seemed to be filled with pictures, newspaper clippings and more small boxes. The room was clean, though sparsely furnished and what was there, looked as though it had been there for as long as she had lived in this crude cabin. The floor was a hard packed surface of soil and I could see the brush streaks where she had swept it recently. My feet were beginning to cramp from the cold emanating from the earth.

Good heavens, it's only September and the floor is this cold, what's it like in January, how can she live here like this? Going to the pot bellied stove I held my hand near it, ice cold, no wonder she's sick. She must have been too sick to even build a fire.

Going out to the woodpile I grabbed an armload of split wood chunks and hurried back to the frigid cabin. Looking around for paper to crumple up to start the fire, I spotted an old piece of newspaper lying on a chair. Grabbing it I headed for the stove.

She came bounding off that sofa, snatched the paper from my hand, put it back where I found it and pointed toward a kindling box in the corner.

She almost collapsed from the effort, but her precious paper was safe.

When I had the fire roaring I banked the stove and covered her with a brightly woven blanket that I found stashed in a box by her bed. Patting her hand I told her I would be back in the morning.

Driving home, regretting that I couldn't do more to help Mina, I vowed I would see to it that she had a decent burial in the cemetery she loved so much. She would have a marble headstone that reads "Here Lies Mina Mallory, dedicated to the end."

I woke early Wednesday morning feeling depressed and a little wary of what I would find when I got to Mina's house. I pushed myself to shower and dress, made my coffee and picked up rolls. I tried to act like this was another normal day of research, but my mind kept telling me this wasn't going to be business as usual. I parked my car in my usual spot, walked to the place by the oil drum, set my thermos down and started toward the cabin Mina calls home.

The door opened and there was Mina, just as agile as always, her quirky little smile filling her wrinkled face with the light of wellbeing.

"See, I told ya Morning Star's potion would make me better. Now come on we gotta get ta work, the onlyest thing growin' now is them dam weeds. Taint yer day but we missed yesterday so it'll be alright."

I was in complete shock. I was expecting to find her dead body and here she was spry as her friend the fieldmouse. I followed her to the patch of ground that had become her life.

The leaves were drifting down and settling in the sunken earth, creating golden blankets. Red leaves were tossed in the gentle breeze touching here, twisting there and turning until they came to rest as though choosing its place of adornment.

She smiled, "Won't have ta weed today. "Mother Earth" is takin' care of em. We can sit a spell and visit with the people, they git awful lonesome in the fall and winter."

She always expected me to remember where she left off and give her a subtle hint, which I did. "Mina did it take long for you and Henry to get together?"

"Naw, me an Henry was really somethin' back then, we spent a lotta time in the woods behind Pap's farm, we walked, talked, and made love everday. I wish we coulda went on like that forever. Pap took ta watchin' me, but I was too full of Henry ta see. When he did catch us it was too late, I was with child. Pap gave me such a whippin' that I thought fer sure I would lose that baby, but I didn't. Pap went ta Gray Wolf and they decided we should be married for the sake of the child.

"The Shaman refused to perform the ceremony so we went ta the minister and he said it weren't right ta marry outa yer race. Here we are, in love, gonna have a child, wantin' ta marry, an' no one ta say the words!

"Talk got round bout me an' Henry an folks started starin' an pointin' fingers at me. I begged Henry ta pack up an' move away from these vultures but no, he said it would be the same everwhere we go, gotta stay an' face it.

"Pap said folks been lookin' purty funny at him an Moses when they go inta town, started callin' them injun lovers, an a few other choice names. Ma and him talked it over an accepted that I should move ta the camp with Henry. I was more then ready ta do that, be with my love everday an night. Who could ask fer more?

"The day I went ta join Henry the whole tribe was waitin', when I got down from the wagon they all turned their backs ta me, they were rejectin' me as a member.

"Pap's jaw got hard like it always did when he was mad. He gave the horses a snap with the whip an' drove off leavin' me with Henry and a camp full of strangers.

"Henry took my belongin's inta the leanto he built outta wood and brush surrounded by barren ground. It looked like a hard wind would blow it over, but it stood through many a storm both inside and out. 'You must prove yourselves to the tribe before they will accept us, they don't hold with mixing blood,' Henry explained.

"Our first night together was heaven on earth, but the mornin' was hell! I woke and went to fix my lover's food.

"The woman of the tribe pushed close together so there was no room to get to the campfire.

"I next went to the stream to get water fer drinkin' and the woman brought the children and bathed them where I was fillin' my ladle. I begged them ta give us a chance, but they threw scornful looks at me an' kept on washin' the children as though I wern't even there.

"Henry had worked laying track fer the railroad once and thought this would make a difference when he went ta find work in the white mans world. But nobody wanted ta hire a lazy, no count injun, and they told him so. He had ta be content with huntin' and doing some woman's work, buildin' the campfire was one job I was glad ta hand over ta him. Never did like messin' with fire. I learned, if I got up while it was still dark and fetched my water fer drinkin', the water was clear and fresh, not cloudy from sand and salt used in the bathin'. The onlyest time it were'nt hard is when we was in our lean-to, close to each other.

"When my time came Henry went ta Morning Star and told her I was ready. She stared long an' hard, then took her bag of geegaws an came ta me. My labor was terrible but she warned me not ta cry out, 'You gotta out do yer sisters of the tribe, you gotta be braver and stronger than any of us.'

"When the child came, he came ina rush a blood an' screams, his not mine. I was too wore out ta do anythin' cept stare at him. That beautiful child came otta me. I felt so proud!

"Henry came inta the leanto, took the bloody screamin' child an went out in the cold dawn, held him high fer all ta see an declared, 'He is a member of the People an always will be.'

"That was the beginnin' of my acceptance. We still needed someone ta step forward ta be his name giver, but I learned there was no hurry. We had a year or so ta name the child.

"In the world of the white man we named the child right away, not carin' if the name fits the child or not.

"The People wait until a name giver gets a sign or has a dream bout the child an' names him after that dream.

"When Henry's mother was six months old a name giver had a dream that she was walkin' under the mornin' star and that is why he named her Morning Star. Gray Wolf, same thing, his namegiver saw a gray wolf while dozin' by a camp fire, he never really knew if it was real or a dream, but he named Henry's father jist in case it was a dream."

While she talked I compared her life to mine. What an ungrateful person I had become. I wondered if I would have remained as dedicated to my family.

"That was a hard winter but we managed ta scratch tagether enough ta eat an keep us warm. I was nursin' the child so needed more food then normal. I knowed Henry went without ta make sure I had enough ta eat. He went huntin' everday but even the game was sparse. The others cooked in a big pot in the center of the camp, but we still weren't allowed to share the food. He didn't say anythin', but I could see the hurt in his eyes. He'd always been a part of his people an' now, cause of me, he was on the outside. He never blamed me fer the spot we were in, but I did.

"I knowed if he'd a chose one of the tribe fer his wife he would still be in with The People.

"When a member of the tribe takes a wife he can move inta the tipi with his wife's parents, but Henry lost his standin' with the tribe. He wasn't shunned he was on the outside lookin' in on many of the rituals.

"That winter came tearin' in on a storm and was the coldest one in many a year. Even the game foraged for food only when starvin'.

"The General Store got broken inta a coupla times that winter an' a course they blamed the 'No count injuns.' Tweren't them, but try an git anybody ta listen. Henry took ta makin' spruce beer ta sell an' it did bring in enough ta provide some staples for the kip. The men from town would come under cover of darkness ta buy the beer.

"One time he was out huntin' an saw two white men in a field butcherin' a steer. They called him over and handed him a front quarter, an said 'if you say anythin' we're gonna say you did it an we caught you, so ya might as well share some of the beef.' Henry didn't want ta keep it but he didn't have a choice, he had me an' the child ta feed an it was the first meat we had fer over a month.

"When he came inta camp with the meat slung over his shoulder, the people stopped what they were doin' an' stared. Henry told the tribe how he got the meat; he didn't want them to think he stole the white man's food. That could bring down shame an' vengeance on the people.

"I remember one child in particular that hung onta his mother's leggin', eyes big starin' at the beef. His mother's eyes never left Henry's face, her look silently pleadin' for her child. Henry walked to the pot hangin' over the community fire, squatted an strippin' the skin from the prize, handed it ta Old Walking Stick, the oldest of the tribe. She turned ta face the north, lifted the skin in the air an' sang in some tongue that I never did learn. Soon others joined her in dancin' an singin'. I learned later that God gives all food, an' must be thanked.

"Now, we said thanks fer our food at home but never so joyfully, I made up my mind right then an' there that I liked the People's way better.

"Most times the families had their own fires by their tipi, an the woman would cook the meal, but in hard times it was wiser ta cook in the public pot ta make sure that the whole tribe would survive. When Henry was done cuttin' up the meat inta small chunks so's they'd cook fast, he dumped them inta the pot an' came an' stood by me. Morning Star came an stood on the left, Gray Wolf thought bout it fer a long time an finally moved forward ta stand by his wife.

"Old Walking Stick took the skin an' put it inta the fire, she took off her moccasins an rubbin' some ointment on her shriveled old feet she took coals from the fire.

"Her head thrown back she chanted a few words an' touched her feet with the coals. At first the beauty of her chant froze me, then I saw that she was burnin' herself. I started forward ta stop her but Henry grabbed my arm.

" 'No, she is usin' a fire charm, an sacrificin' her comfort for payment of the stolen food. She will be all right if her sacrifice is accepted.'

" But ya didn't steal the food an' we do need it so bad."

" 'That is not a reason to take what belongs to others, I must make my peace with Creator too' "

"Well, I hope yer not gonna burn yerself or ruin any part of that beautiful body, that's all.

"When the ritual was done so was the food an we all ate. Old Walking Stick wandered over ta where we were settin' an' I asked how her feet were an' did they hurt very much? She chuckled an' took of her moccasins.

"They were as wrinkled as her body but there wern't a burn or scar on her feet. Henry said the Creator had accepted her prayer offerin'.

"Well, let me tell ya that was the best food we ett in a long time.

"I'd long ago stopped makin' milk for the child. Not enough food I reckon, an' was feedin' him corn gruel ta fill his belly. This was the baby's first real meal an' he ett like a little pig. When he was full, his daddy gave him a bone ta chaw on.

"The teeth were 'bout ta break through an' bitin' on the bone helped. Ta finish the meal Morning Star gave baby a small cake of maple syrup an blackberries hardened with elk fat that she'd saved for his name givin,' but thought he should have it now. His dark little eyes shone with such pleasure. We tucked him back in his cradle fer the night an' I sang lullabies to him till his eyes couldn't stay open anymore. He was such a beautiful child!"

She knelt and began to weed with such fury that I thought she would collapse from a stroke. When she recovered somewhat she began to relate a story that even the townsfolk didn't talk about.

"Two days later, Gray Wolf led a scoutin' party out an most of the young men were off lookin' fer game. Henry an' some of the older braves stayed ta guard the camp. Mornin' came and the sounds of the wind howlin' through ever' nook an' cranny of the hut woke me with its whine.

"Over the sounds of the wind came the steady beat of horses crashin' through the woods. Henry an' me weren't the only folks that heard it. The whole camp was stirrin' round an' lookin' ta see what was happenin'.

"The men rode in carrin' torches, spewin' curses an' shoutin' 'bout thievin' injuns stealin' from honest white folks an thinkin' they were gonna git away with it! They came roarin' in with guns an' whips, shootin' and slashin' everbody in sight.

"I grabbed the baby an' ran through the fire that was eatin' our home.

"Hidin' under the closest pine tree that had its branches close ta the ground, I watched as those men torched the whole village. Old Walking Stick never did move from her tipi, she set in the center and watched as the deerskin cover burned 'round her. Her eyes closed an' I thought she was sayin' prayers, but we found out later that she died settin' there watchin' her home go up in flames.

"Henry tried ta drag one of the men offen his horse, but instead got smashed in the head from a riffle butt, his head split open, the blood that shot out of his wound washed his face in the red reflection of the blazin' fires. His face was so filled with hate that I could understand the fear most folks felt for the Indian. If I didn't know him I woulda feared him too."

She was silent for quite a while, her hands that usually were busy pulling weeds, smoothing bumpy ground, and patting the sunken earth, were suddenly very still; she sat as though frozen in the past.

"Peekin' out from the branches of the tree, I looked 'round the camp, the tipis was all gone, gone, burnt ta pieces, the poles stood like skeletons in the cold gray mornin'. The horses were shot or run off.

"The raiders even trampled the dogs. We counted on the dogs for meat if the game got too sparse an' now they were gone.

She spoke in a whisper. "The pot that hung over the camp fire was layin' on its side, the precious food spillin' on the frozen ground."

Dear God, who could blame her for hurting even after all these years, dead of winter, no home, no food, her man wounded and a child to care for.

Many times Mina worked in complete silence and I bided my time waiting for her to relate another of her remembrances. I often found myself pulling weeds and brushing away fallen branches from the many oaks and birch trees that surrounded the small, secluded cemetery. Mina would look up, see me, nod her head, and continue ministering to the people of her world.

My mind would wander to my own daughter, Jamie Lee, named after her father, a composite of Jim and I, and the love we had shared. My brown eyes, her father's vibrant personality and gorgeous auburn hair.

Her supple figure and smooth tan skin attests to many hours on tennis courts and beaches. She has zest for life, always smiling, gentle, and loving. I don't remember being that young and so full of life.

Mina often hummed some forgotten tune, but the melody stirred up pictures of Pow Wows, hunters stalking deer in fields of golden grain, women washing clothes in sparkling streams, and soft nights under a star filled sky.

I felt such longing for something that I had never experienced, or had I? The people say a soul lives on. Did I perhaps live in another time and place? Is that what led me here to this nearly abandoned cemetery in the middle of nowhere?

I learned to appreciate the time spent with Mina, and her gentle ways. The quiet afforded me time to look deep within and discover the lost child, the person that I had buried in this busy, hectic world.

"When those men finished their wreckin' the camp, they rode off laughin' and pattin' each other on the back, boastin' how brave they were. Well, I knowed how brave they really were an' I was achin' let my family know 'bout the burnin' an' whippin' of helpless old women an' children.

"The only men that were in camp that mornin' were beaten, wounded or dead.

"Holdin' the cradle close ta my breast, I pushed myself outta the branches an' ran ta where Henry was layin'; eyes closed an' pale as death. I did think he was dead at first, but with my touch to his face his eyes opened an' in em I saw fear for the first time."

Her shoulders shook as she silently wept for the loss of her brave, fearless Henry.

"He never was the same after that. Henry did tell me later that the men that gave him the meat rode with that band of men that did that awful thing ta us.

"There we were in the camp that couldn't protect us, without food an' sure ta be accused of rustlin' that steer. The people wandered 'round in a daze, their hopes stolen by thieves in the frozen dawn. I wanted ta go ta town an' tell everybody what happened out here but Henry said, 'No it won't do no good, it'd make things worse.' How could things be worse then what it is right now?

"It was decided we must move on ta safer huntin' grounds, but first we needed ta take care of our wounded and dead. Henry said no when I tried ta tend his wound, so I helped the women of the tribe git Old Walking Stick ready for the buryin' ritual by gatherin' birch bark ta wrap the gifts she would take ta the land of the departed.

" 'Twas the way of the people ta wrap food an' her favorite cookin' tools in the bark, but there weren't no food and all her things were gone, so I didn't have ta gather much. The other women washed her body, braided her hair, an' painted her face, as was the custom.

"The fires had ta burn for three days ta thaw the earth so a grave could be dug.

"One after another her brothers an sisters of the tribe came and took turns settin' next ta her body an' advisin' her ta be careful an' ta avoid certain paths after each warnin' they hit the drum ta make sure she heeded it."

As I listened to Mina relate this horrifying part of her life I wondered if I would have been able to survive this ordeal and remain sane.

"The tipi poles that weren't burned were gathered, stacked and tied for travel, all 'cept the poles from Old Walking Stick's tipi. Those can't never be used again cause she died in her tipi. The ashes from the fires were stomped out and brushed inta the earth. The people believe that a campsite must be returned ta the way it was afore they settled there.

"The children were hungry an' fretful waitin' fer their elders ta finish their tribute ta the earth.

"The one an' only horse that was left was kilt an' prepared for the long trek north ta another place where we would be safe. The cold did make it easier ta store the meat while on the trail. A sled was made from branches and some of the deerskin that wasn't burned in the fire. We didn't have a horse ta pull it so the women of the tribe would take turns haulin' the heavy load, an they had ta tote the tipi poles too. Those that didn't have children in cradles on their back carried the bundles of wood ta the next camp.

"Henry was strangely quiet. The others were grumblin' as they worked, but he just looked at them through unseein' eyes.

"At long last we were on our way north toward the rushin' waters of the big falls. The trek was torture for the tribe but bettern stayin' where we were an' bein' shot or starvin' ta death.

"That first day on the trail was the meanest cause the children never had ta face such brutal treatment an' now they were faced with the lesson of survival without food an' rest. The people spoil their children, they are never allowed ta cry; they are tutored ta in every way till they are growed. This made it awful hard for them.

"When night come on us we stopped long side a frozen stream. We broke through the layers of ice an' dipped fresh water inta the gourds that carried our drinkin' water. Drinking lotta water helps fill the empty belly. One of the women come forward with the food from the ground back at the camp. She'd scrapped it up for the children to eat along the way. It was grainy from earth being mixed with it but the children had full bellies agin that night."

40

Chapter Three

"I thanked God everday fer the patience that the other women showed in this terrible time of our lives. They put their trust in the Mide Manido (Grand Medicine Spirit). This is the closest they came to namin' our God.

"We foraged for roots, dried berries still hangin' on the bush, boiled birch bark to make a broth. Pine needles an' birch bark boiled together make a spicy drink ta fool the belly inta thinkin' its food.

"The braves that were able hunted ahead fer game an' a safe restin' place. I thought that trek would never end. They came back empty handed, there was no critters ta be found. The forth night on the trail was bitter cold an' there was no way our dribble of food an' shelter could carry us much longer.

"We huddled together fer warmth, puttin' the children inside the circle of our bodies. Bein' bone tired an' weak we slept till dawn.

"Henry was the first ta rise, he shook me an' smilin' raised his arms ta the sky. Sometime durin' the night the wind had changed an' the heat of the sun was warmin' the earth.

"It was like spring in the middle of winter. It was as if we were all born agin inta a new world.

"The children stopped whinin' an' ran ta play with the few toys they had left; the men got ready ta hunt; the women gathered wood an' built a fire for the food that would surely be found. "Mide Manido" was watchin' over us.

"The critters in the forest must have felt the same way cause one of the braves come across rabbits playin' in a clearin', another brave saw a doe nibblin' on grass that the sun bared from the snow. Well I mean ta tell ya, we were all happy ta pitch in an' git the meat ready fer cookin' an' puttin' some away fer the rest of the trek. The three rabbits went inta the pot an' the doe was cut inta sections, partly dried on a frame over the campfire so it would keep for the journey. The innards were used fer holdin' the tallow.

"I had much ta learn, but I was always there to watch an' help.

"That fine weather lasted fer three days an' gave us a chance ta build up our strength an' store enough food fer the rest of the trek. A terrible storm hit us on the trail, whippin' 'round our bodies an' tearin' at our clothes as we walked ta our new home. When the day was half gone, Gray Wolf called a halt ta the trek; we were near some tall hills of sand that would give us protection from the cuttin', slashin' wind. We hurried ta the shelter of the mounds of earth an' sand an' hunkered down ta wait out the storm.

"The blowin' sand from the dunes was as cuttin' as the wind, but it was warmer there an' ya could always turn yer back ta the wind."

Mina's description of the trek and the vicious storm that attacked during the move to another camp was so vivid that I felt as though I was there. My mouth was dry from the sand and wind that was ripping at these desperate people.

I felt anger and guilt at the unfair treatment of these innocent human beings forced to move from their home in the dead of winter.

I swore to myself that I would find a way to amend this terrible wrong.

Nothing could make up for the inhuman treatment they had received, but there had to be a way to vindicate the tribe from being viciously labeled thieves.

"The storm raged on through the night an' the people tried ta sleep out its fury. Mornin' came an' we were able ta git a small fire started. We all needed food to give us strength fer the rest of the trek. Since it weren't a real good day ta travel it was decided ta take the baths we all were needin', it'd been a while since any one had a bath an' all were feelin' pretty itchy. The people were used ta washin' themselves regularly an' a bath was way over due. Snow was gathered, put ina pot an' the fire was fed ta keep it burnin'. A few big stones was found an' put inta the fire ta heat, they were pulled out and put inta the pot. When the water was hot people came with their pot an' ladles, takin' the water; they went ta bath their children, while more water was heated. When the children were done the pots was filled again fer the adults ta bath. Most went off ta some private place ta wash but some of the old ones stayed near the fire, their mate or child holdin' up a blanket fer privacy."

This last part of the story was told to me over a period of two weeks and in short bursts of unusual wordiness. Mina told it with such clarity that I felt as though I were there sharing the bitter cold and hunger with her and her people.

"Jist as soon as the bad weather let up, we headed for the camp grounds that Gray Wolf had heard about from his father, Ravens Wing. He said it was a perfect place ta camp, game was plentiful, the falls never froze, so there was fresh water all year an' the valley near by was sheltered from the storms.

"I thought ta myself, if it's so perfect why did the people live in that other camp? When I said this ta Morning Star, she hunched her shoulders an' said, " 'We need ta be near our fathers, mothers, an' friends that have gone on ta the other side.' "

"When we finally got to the place of encampment, another tribe was already settled there.

"Another Ojibway tribe was campin' fer the winter. They welcomed us an' planned a feast ta celebrate our safe journey. The camps were friendly with each other an' the rest of the winter months slid by. The young men of the tribe spent most of their time huntin', fishin', an' buildin' canoes ta cross the lake that stood between the island an' this spot.

"In the spring the first Ojibway tribe decided ta journey further north across the big waters, they invited us ta come 'long but it was decided that we would linger there for the summer.

"Sometimes in the evenin' when the work was done an' the child was sleepin', I would think bout my family back at the other place where we camped. I now remember them as strangers I usta know ina dream. I guess the townsfolk were right. I did turn injun.

"Our days were spent workin', fishin', preservin', pickin' berries an' dryin' em fer the winter, an' mendin' clothes, but our evenin's was spent learnin' new things an listenin' ta the tales the old ones told the children. There were three kinds of stories, one 'bout the first earth an' its inhabitants, then there was some 'bout adventures an' doin's of "Wi nabo jo" (the master of life), an' the (a dizo'ke) fairy tales which were told jist fer the childrens delight.

"Morning Star showed me how ta make clothes from skins of animals that Henry hunted an' trapped. I specially liked makin' the little moccasins for baby, they were simple an' I could trim them with beads an' paint pictures on them. I lined them with rabbit fur to keep his feet warm. He loved it when I had his feet bare to try on new moccasins.

"That's when we played bite the toes an' he would giggle out loud. Henry loved the game as much as baby, sometimes I hada make him stop or baby got so worked up he couldn't sleep fer hours."

Mina fell silent for the longest time and her shoulders shook in agony. I didn't urge her to speak. I sensed the deep hurt that was tearing at her very essence.

My Jim came to mind while I was waiting for Mina to find release from her torment. I asked myself if I had given as much of myself as Mina had, would we still be together?

That was something that I would never find out as the divorce was final and the die had been cast. Mina was made of stronger stuff than I.

"One spring mornin' a stranger showed up at the village. He'd been trappin' round the area an' had a sled fulla skins he was haulin' ta the tradein' post in Mackinaw. He wanted ta trade some skins fer a canoe. We didn't have a extra canoe an' we didn't need skins as the men had a good season too. A bargain was struck for beads an' cloth, the cookin' pans he carried were part of the bargain too. The young men petitioned the official canoe maker ta build one for the trapper. They offered ta help him by doin' the hard work while he set the size an' did the measurin'.

"The canoe maker is very important ta the tribe. The welfare an' safety of the tribe depend on the skill an' experience of a good canoe maker. Gray Fox told the stranger if the official canoe maker of the tribe would build one fer him an' the young men of tribe helped then he could pay fer it with stories of his adventures.

"The people were always hungry ta hear new tales an' news of other tribes in the area. They would set round the campfire and listen ta the same stories over an' over, sometimes they would ask questions an' laugh at the endless answers. We liked ta see the hunters an' trappers that dropped inta the camp cause they brought us news, beads, sometimes cloth ta trade, an' tole us wild tales of their hunt.

"The bad part was they sometimes gave us sickness that we couldn't cure. This trapper stayed the six days it took ta build the canoe an left early on the mornin' of the seventh.

"The next evenin' baby got a cough that tore through his whole body, he was burnin' up with fever. Nothin' Morning Star give him seemed ta help, we washed him in cold water, wrapped him in skins ta sweat the fever out, give him magic potions till he wouldn' open his little mouth anymore.

"Come dawn of the fifth day of the sickness, the namegiver came an' told me he had a dream.

"He saw the baby walk hand in hand inta the other land with Old Walking Stick. I knowed by this time what that meant; he was here ta give the baby a name before he died.

"I set still watchin' while he performed the name giver rite.

"It is said that sometimes the given of a name made the child get better, I wanted ta believe it but I couldn't. He took the child in his arms and gave him the name "Ce' nawickunji" (he produces a rattling sound with the movement of his being). The people told me if I believed that the Great Power could give back life, he would. I hada hard time tryin' ta believe that cause I saw how sick the child was.

" 'If you hear thunder he will live, if you don't he will die' he told me an' Henry. Makin' the child a spirit bundle is part of the child's history; it holds his favorite toy, pieces of clothin', his blanket, leggin's with beads trimmin' the sides, an' a piece of his hair, most things he will need on the other side.

"I stood there in the tipi clutchin' the child's spirit bundle, all my senses strainin' ta hear thunder. I could smell the fire from the hardwood pieces that was burnin' outside, the musky odor of the skins that hung on the rack, an' the sweat from our bodies from long nights carin' fer the child. I was strainin' with ever muscle in my body ta hear the least sound of thunder, ever sound was bigger, I swear I could hear the trees whisperin' ta each other.

"Did I hear the thunder? I don't know if that loud sound was thunder or my blood thunderin' through my veins.

"I cain't 'xplain it but the child stopped thrashin' round. He laid so still; it was the first time in many days. He was sleepin'.

"I started ta believe. I set up all night an' watched the child rest. Henry slept the sleep of the believer.

"In the mornin' both of them was rested an' ready ta take on the world, but I was so tired I stayed in the tipi until the sun was straight up. I didn't sleep but I was restin' an' thankin' both his god and mine fer the life of my son.

"The many stories I heard from the women as we worked, came back ta me as I lay thinking of the last few days.

"They told me of many strange things that happened in their fathers' time, belief that people can assume the form that they were in a nother life.

"Its said the power of the dream was so great that a man was known ta assume the form that had been his in a previous existence and became the subject of his dreams. One of the tales was bout a brave that was wounded an' his body disappeared, in its place appeared a coyote that got up an' ran away. The brave's body was never found. When they first told me the story I jist listened an' thought they were tellin' ghost stories like we use ta do back when I was a child. After what I saw last night I knowed there was more ta these stories then what I thought."

I had a difficult time accepting what Mina had told me, but she believed it so that was all that was important. I was sure she thought she had given me all the facts, but there had to be a better explanation than the simple act of giving of a name to save a child's life.

Mina had begun inviting me into her home on occasion and she also began to share the information that she had saved over the years. Some of the clippings were obituaries of men that she claimed helped in the raid that dreadful night.

There was no expression on her face when she showed me, but her eyes twinkled and I knew for sure that she didn't morn for them.

Taking a box from a corner of the small room she carefully held up a ragged clipping that had been torn from an aged sheet of newspaper.

"This here tells the white man's story of the killin' an' burnin' of our homes that terrible time, so many years ago."

The article read as follows: It was reported that on early Sunday morning of last week, while the good folks of the town were sleeping or getting ready to attend the services at the local meeting house, a band of three drunken Indians raided Silas Roth's herd of steers.

They had been sheltered in a lean-to on his farm, but somehow had wandered into the open field in search of grass. The thieves had slaughtered two of his prize steer and left the remains out in the open to taunt the owner. Toady Joe, one of the men from town, had passed that way and saw the Indians, but was out numbered, so fearing for his life he rode into town. He decided to wait until later that morning to tell the sheriff about the whole episode because it was early and everyone was asleep.

While this wasn't very prudent on his part, there was no harm done and he did say it was too late to save the animals anyhow. Later that Sunday afternoon a few men rode out to the camp and spoke to the Chief. He admitted that a couple of his young braves committed this thievery and promised the sheriff he would take retribution. The accusations surely must have been true because a week later when the sheriff rode out to see how the chief had punished the braves, the whole tribe had moved. Seems to me that a lynching would be the appropriate answer to the problem of Indians stealing from a good Christian farmer. Hang one and the rest learn a much-deserved lesson.

I was shaking with an anger that consumed my whole body, what an unmitigated lie! How dare they conceal the action of a mob of killers?

Mina just shrugged her shoulders and said, "What will be, will be, cain't change it now." She sat very still and gazed out the window, into the woods, lost in her reverie, hopefully dreaming of happier times with the gentle people.

"Did I ever tell ya how the People believe the world was made? No? Well sir, it were in the beginning, Nan-a-po-sho, (the great spirit), made the otter, the beaver, the musk-rat, and a fox, course that there world was all water.

"The otter was chosen ta search for some sign of green growin things. Bein proud ta be chosen first he went down into the water searchin for some kinda solid land. Went down three times and didn't find even a grain of sand. The wore out otter fell dead at the feet of Nan-a-po-sho.

"The beaver was picked next and he done the same thing and fell dead from exhaustion. Then came the musk-rat an he dived inta the water and he did bring up a goodly pile of sand, but he worked real hard to git it. Yup, you got it right, he died too.

"Nan-a-po-sho brushed all the sand inta a pile and told the fox ta run around it an spread the sand with his tail until it was a big island an it took up hundreds of acres.

"Nan-a-po-sho decided the land needed a bein an so he took pieces of the dead animals an addin his own spit an blood an hair, he made man.

"The man's job was ta take care of the squash, corn, an tobacco that grew on the land. The man worked hard, but he was lonely.

"With a few pieces of the musk-rat, parts of the fish an a bone taken from the shoulder of the man, he made a women to help plant, skin his musk-rats, an carry his burdens. They say that the mans shoulder bone made the woman stronger an is the reason the woman was created, ta do the heavy labor.

"Ain't much different then what the preacher told us when I was a child, specially bout the spittin part.

"Did ya ever see a mama spit on a rag an gently clean her child's face? The look in the child's eyes, all lovin, an so wrapped up in his mama. Now, don't that seem kinda god like?"

Last December was the last time we were at the small graveyard in the woods together. It was one of those rare winter days when a blanket of snow covered all the imperfections of a less than perfect world.

God's cleansing mantle of white had turned the cemetery into a quiet, restful place to be.

As we stood with the warmth of the sun washing our face, a chipmunk scurried through the unmarked snow leaving a jigsaw pattern in its wake. It was so peaceful.

I looked at the face of my friend Mina and was awed by the beauty on her face, I saw the girl, I saw the love, and I saw her soul. I felt as though I was in the presence of God. In that moment a strange serenity enveloped me and I knew I would never be afraid again.

When we were finally able to tear ourselves away from the sanctuary in the pines, and headed back toward Mina's place. She suddenly dropped to the ground and lay still.

I knew that she was overcome with exhaustion and her poor diet certainly didn't help matters. Walking quickly back to my car where I grabbed a blanket and rushed back to the still body of Mina. Covering her lifeless form I whispered, "I'll go and get help, be right back."

"Ya don't hafta worry none, I ain't dyin' yet, got too much work ta do ta leave right now. Gotta make sure ya got the whole story fore I kin git some peace!"

My heart was breaking. This wonderful little old lady was worried about my feelings and my story, even at a time like this.

Running back to my car and driving like a crazy woman, I made my way to the closest farm, which was about five miles a way.

A woman answered my frantic beating on the door. She looked a little frightened but, when I hastily explained why I was there the woman stepped aside and motioned toward the phone sitting on the stand in the hall.

The one and only ambulance was on a run to an auto accident out on the highway and I should bring her right in as it sounded like a stroke and that needed immediate attention.

I hurried back to my friend lying in the woods and half carried and half dragged her to my car in the clearing. Carefully placing her in the back seat I headed toward Standish and the nearest hospital.

The doctor in emergency took one look at Mina and immediately ordered an IV.   The nurse had a difficult time finding a vein in which to insert the needle.   Mina lay very still her dark eyes watching every move, but not making a sound.

I could see in her every small gesture the essence and bearing of a woman that has borne great hardships and learned to accept and survive them.   I was proud to be her friend.

There was a big hassle about her having no insurance, and the charity ward being filled to capacity.   I became very annoyed with the billing clerk and told them to bill me.

Just as soon as she was settled into her room, she winked at me and said, "They don't know it yet, but they owe me this room an' then some."

Medication, I thought, making her say things she doesn't mean.   Little did I know that in a few short weeks I would find out how much we all owed her.

The following day I went to the hospital to visit Mina. Stopping at the desk to ask how she was doing, I was shocked to find out she had left sometime during the night.   When the nurse went in to give her sleep medication, she was gone.

Mina, Mina, why do you do these things to make me worry I grumbled as left the hospital?   Then I realized that I had taken it upon myself to decide what was best for someone, who obviously was able to make decisions for herself.

She knew where and how she wanted to spend the rest of her life. I had no right to fault her for that.

On my way to the only place I knew she would be, I promised myself to accept her just as she is.

"Come on in, I knowed you'd be here." She hollered.

I pushed open the door, and saw her huddled on the fallen down sofa, a warm blanket was spread over her small frame. Her hair was flowing around her shoulders giving her the allusion of youth. She was where she had to be.

I went to the only chair in the room and carefully moved the newspapers that were stacked there.

Placing them on top of a box along side the chair, I sat down and waited for Mina to speak.

"Ain't got yer tablet! No matter, ya ain't gonna fergit what I'm bout ta tell ya anyway.

"The years we spent at the new camp were magic, me an Henry had 'nother son, we had him named right away, I weren't takin' no chances. A travelin' preacher came through that second year an I talked him inta marrin' me an Henry, he said it sure needed doing since we had two children together.

"Them summers nights were warm an' food was right outside our tipi. The whole tribe was content fer the first coupla years.

"Yes sir, we had some wonderful years in that new camp, but tradition dies hard, 'specially with the old ones. At the end of our fourth summer there, the elders in the tribe begun ta mumur bout bein' buried in ground that ain't sacred. The trees round the camp started ta die; a strange bug was suckin' the life outta them. When we ate the fish, they made us sick. The old ones said these was signs that we should move back ta our valley.

"Little Thunder, that was what we called our first born, was four summers old an runnin' an playin' with the other children in the tribe an I now was accepted an' treated the same as any other member of the tribe. I hated ta leave that place where we was so happy.

"The birthin' of Small Turtle weren't as hard as the first but all of the women of the tribe was there for me, offerin' advice an some even gave me little gifts for the child. It was the happiest time of my life. I took up the pipe after Small Turtle was born an' settled right inta smokin' it regular like the rest of the women.

"The council decided we was ta move back ta the camp by the Titabawassee. We spent weeks getting ready for the trek.

"I sensed the difference in Henry right away. The old anger that was buried was comin' ta the top again an' I feared what might happen. I talked ta Morning Star bout her son's anger, my fears an' she jist nodded.

54

Chapter Four

"It was a joyous trek back, the winds was calm, the leaves was turnin' all brown an gold, small creatures were scurrin' round storin' their food for winter.

"When we reached our old campsite, it was changed. The trees were gone, cut down by the woodsman's axe, an' the land was plowed, empty cornstalks were standin' in rows waitin' ta be plowed under. Anger flashed on Gray Wolf's face, 'This is our land. They can't do this, somebody made a mistake. I must see the sheriff about this.

"Gray Wolf , I pleaded let me go talk ta the sheriff bout the mistake, after all I was one of their own people, an' I was sure the sheriff would listen ta me.

"After much coaxin' an' 'splainin' both Henry an' Gray Wolf agreed that I could go.

"Thunder Cloud, the medicine man, was the only one agin it. He said he saw bad trouble when he shook the bones an' his dreams was filled with trouble. I wouldn't listen. I figured he didn't want women ta do man work. We made camp long side the plowed field an' I got ready ta go inta town.

"Now ya remember I ain't been ta town in years an' sure was surprised at how much it growed. The sheriff's office useta be in the middle of town an' now it was gone.

"I wandered' inta Mr. Schmidt's General Store an' it was twice as big an' filled with all kinds of new things, purty cloth, ropes of beads, an' in a jar on the counter was my favorite, peppermint candy sticks. If I woulda hada few coins I woulda bought a stick fer my sons, but there's no need fer money, when ya live like we do."

"Mr. Schmidt didn't know who I was till I told him. Ya'da thought he woulda knowed me by my red hair, but he didn't. When I asked where the sheriff's office moved ta, he squinted his eyes an' stared at me like he never saw a woman afore. When I told him I was Mina Mallory he shook his head like he didn't believe me. Well, let me tell ya, I didn't change that much, so it musta been somethin' wrong in his head.

"Mrs. Schmidt come outta the back jist as I said my name an' she got this look on her face like she smelled somethin' bad, snickered her long nose, turned round an' headed back where she come from. Her bony back was straight as the ramrods the braves use ta load their rifles. I straightened my shoulders, held my head up high an' marched right outta that durn store. I could find the sheriff without that kind helpin' me.

"Down at the end of the street on a old gray buildin' was a sign that said sheriff Office. Well I hotfooted it down there. I wanted ta git my business over with an' git outta this town. It was chokin' me. I went inta his office an' spoke ta the man settin' behind the desk. He was a fat toady looking man with gray greasy hair and rotten teeth. His eyes held all the meanness in the world. I told him who I was an' what I was there fer. He listened with a smirk pasted on his face an' when I was finished talkin,' he laughed, an said, 'Do ya really think I'm gonna arrest a good law abidin' citizen on the word of an injun lover?

" ' I know what piece of property yer talkin' bout an' that was confiscated for the two steers that you people stole from Silas Roth. He claimed it an' he's workin' it. Now if you people can prove that land is yers then you better have written proof, otherwise it's his ta do what he wants.'

"I showed him the paper that was proof that the land belonged ta the tribe. It was folded in the middle an' it had a pressed seal on the bottom. He looked at it fer a long time an' then he told me it weren't no good cause it was too old, the new deeds were all registered at the land office in a nother town. I asked fer it back. He tore it in half an' handed it back ta me, with a smile. 'That's how much it's worth,' he sniggered."

"My brother Moses lived near here on the other side of town. Decidin' ta visit him an' see if he could help, I walked ta the place I used ta call home.

"A strange woman with a fearful look on her face answered my knockin'. I asked fer Moses an' she told me he was in the field clearin' land fer spring. A youngun hung on ta her skirt, peepin' round his mama's apron. He looked like Moses but had black hair like his mama. I told her who I was an' she didn't even invite me in. I asked when did she think he would return an she answered, 'When he gits good an' ready!'

"That trip was fer nothin'. I couldn't depend on my family ta help either. I saw my mama peekin' out the window as I headed back fer town. I couldn't blame her, she was dependent on Moses fer her welfare. He must have told her not ta have anythin' ta do with me. So be it.

"With heavy heart at the loss of my family's turnin' me away, I hurried ta join my true family that waited fer me.

"The sun was hot that day so I decided ta walk at the edge of the trees. Makin' my way toward that town of hate I gave thanks fer the gentleness of the people of the tribe. They have taken in strangers, adopted children, an' made blood brothers of strangers an' these folks call them heathens. As I rushed ta be with the people that loved an' cared fer me, I heard a sound in the bushes.

"Knowing that somebody was follerin' me. I started ta run but it was too late. Three of the filthiest men I have ever saw barred my way inta town.

"I tried to git passed them but the biggest one grabbed me an' dragged me inta the trees, the other two follered him laughin' an' smirkin'. I knew I was gonna git a beatin' but I didn't expect what came next.

"The smallest one begged ta be first. He said he would save some fer the rest, but he wanted ta try a squaw woman once in his life. After some arguin' it was decided he would be first ta use my body.

"I fought till I couldn't move an' then I jist laid there an' made my mind go way ta nother place. When I came back ta this world they was gone an' it was night. My whole body ached from the force those three animals had used ta hold me. Washin' the filth offa my body with leaves from a bush growin' nearby an grabbin' a low hangin' branch of a tree I pulled myself up. Straightenin' my stained buckskin jumper I stumbled ta the trunk of the tree an pressed my face agin the moss-covered bark, lettin' the cool, damp, green moss leach away the heat from the whisker burns on my cheeks. I cried fer the loss of my spirit.

"After what seemed like days, I was able ta make my way back ta camp. When I staggered in most of the tribe was waitin'. Henry an' three of the other braves was out searchin'. Gray Wolf had sent them out when I didn't return that same day."

I was furious just listening to Mina's story. God help them when the town finds out. Damn them, I thought, how could they do that to a woman just because she chose a man of a different race! What made those animals think it was all right to violate her?

"The women stood by the fire not movin'. I couldn't read their faces, but I knew I was filthy with dirt an' the touch of those animals on my soul.

"Henry rode in and dismounted. He saw me and knew. Rage filled his face. He changed inta a stranger. He started back toward the horses, his body unbendin', jist as I knew his mind would be. Nobody wanted those men dead more then me, but the safety of the tribe was all I could think about. I had children in this camp an' the towns folk ain't ta be trusted. Even old Big Nose John, the half-breed that hung round the tavern in town didn't trust the white men he drank with. Sometimes they was friendly an' sometimes they ain't."

"I went ta him an' begged him ta talk ta the sheriff bout the attack on me, he shrugged me away an' grabbed the mane of his horse an' buried his face in it. I knew he would give the town one more chance ta do the right thing.

"Morning Star come ta me, 'The war will start now' she whispered as she led me inta her tipi, motioned me ta sit while she poured me sassafras tea in a drinkin' gourd.

"Henry was still full of fury when he went inta town ta talk ta the sheriff bout the terrible thing that happened ta me. When he walked inta the office the sheriff pulled his gun an' arrested him fer rustlin'. Henry tried ta tell him what happened years ago when those steers was killed, but he wouldn't listen. Henry said, he jist kept sayin', 'I knew I'd git you thieven injuns one of these days.'

"The sheriff threw Henry inta the closest cell where he could watch him night an' day. We knew what happened by the time the cell door closed on my beloved Henry, thanks ta Big Nose John an' his signals in the sky.

"Me, Gray Wolf, an' Morning Star went inta town ta try an' talk ta the sheriff. We didn't have much hope of changin' his mind, but we still wanted ta try.

"Henry had kept that rage buried deep inside fer too many years an' this was the final outrage, the violation of his woman. He could take no more!

"The sheriff wouldn't let us inta the cell with Henry cause he didn't trust us not ta help him escape. Standin' outside the cage they had him locked in, we saw a man made of stone; he would not look or speak, his anger an' shame was so great.

"Laughin' the sheriff told us how they was gonna hold a trial an' then hang Henry the next day.

"We argued with the sheriff, tellin' him it was white men that killed the beef, but he wouldn't listen. He jist kept sayin', 'We found the burnt skin an' we have a witness, you jist cain't explain that away. Besides I'd take the word of a white man over any injun, any day.'

"Gray Wolf's look promised many things, some not so pleasant, as he stalked from the jail. We followed him in silence.

"On the trail back ta camp, we was met by ten of the youngest braves wantin' ta know where their brother, Henry, was. Gray Wolf told them what the sheriff said an' they started ta whoop with anger. Henry's father tried ta calm them but it was near impossible. 'Ain't the place ta make war, we'er goin' back ta camp ta make plans.'

"The stupor I was in started ta fade an' I yelled, 'My Henry ain't gonna hang tomorra or any other day!' That started the mad young braves ta whoopin' an' hollerin' agin.

"Gray Wolf waited till the shoutin' stopped then he spoke, 'We cannot permit this ta happen, we must git Henry out of that cage. The honor of our people rests with this wrong. We have done our best ta make things right an' git justice. Now is the time fer action. Tonight we attack the jail an' set my son free. We will hit while it is still night, try not ta kill anybody, but we must protect our honor.' I was so proud of my new father an' mother, Henry's parents.

"The attack went off jist as Gray Wolf wanted, the only person hurt was the deputy, he ended up with a cracked noggin, too bad it didn't knock some sense inta him, but it didn't. He stirred up the whole town tellin' them we was gonna raid it an' kill everbody in it. The men from town gathered at the tavern ta drink some courage an' plan what they was gonna do ta us.

"We made plans ta move back ta the land of the fallin' waters where we had all those years of peace, our families was safe an' we didn't want a war. The white faces had won.

"The whole tribe was on the move soon as the braves left for town. They was supposed ta meet us on the trail with Henry an' that's jist what happened. We shoulda stayed where we was, maybe it woulda saved some lives. It was after dusk when we made camp fer the night, when the crazy, screamin' men attacked. They was shootin' anythin' that moved.

"My two sons was playin' by the fire an' they was the first ta be killed. Henry went wild, screamin' an' usin' his battleaxe like a windmill. Blood was splashin' everwhere; children was cryin' an' callin' fer their mama. The man I hit with the club looked up at me with fear an' I saw the truth flash inta his eyes, jist as I stabbed him in the throat.

"My hands was washed in the blood of one of my violators.

"I fought my way ta my dead children layin' on the cold black ground, all sprawled out like dolls that was throwed away. Little Thunder's hand was in the fire an' I could smell the odor of my son's burnin' flesh.

"I took his meltin' hand an' laid it on his chest. My breast ached with the milk little Turtle couldn't suckle.

"The attack was soon over an' the quiet was unbearable. I lay clutchin' the lifeless bodies of my sons till Morning Star come ta fetch me away from the horror. The moon was shinin' down on the destruction left by the white men. They'd picked up their wounded an' dead an rode off toward town, takin' Henry with them."

"There was only three of us left when the sun come up. Morning Star had a gash on her head that wouldn't stop bleedin'. Small Horse, one of the children, was wanderin' round cryin' fer his mama. His mama's body was partly buried under the lifeless body of Gray Wolf. He had died with honor fightin' the enemy.

"We got our dead ready fer the rite of burial, made up the spirit bundles that had been burned, for the murdered members of the tribe an' prayed those white men wouldn't come back."

Mina's voice broke when she related the part about her murdered children. I tried to put myself in her place and experience her hurt, but I couldn't even imagine it, much less know the emptiness and helplessness she must have felt.

"Well sir, I made up my mind my Henry weren't gonna hang an' that was that, so inta town I went. Morning Star weren't in no shape ta ride an' she had Small Horse ta see ta anyway. I finally coaxed one of the scared horses ta let me git up on his back. I didn't know what I was gonna do but I couldn't jist set there an' do nothin'.

"The braves had tore the bars loose on his cell when they broke him out the first time an' they wrecked half the wall when they did. The bar was still hangin' all crazy from the wooden frame.

"I sneaked up ta the jail pressin' myself agin the wall so's I wouldn't be spotted.

"Callin' his name softly, I inched half way round the buildin' afore I found him. They had Henry locked ina cell in the back of the jail. When I heard his answer low an' sweet, I wanted ta tear the wall away with my bare hands, but I weren't strong nough.

"Henry wanted ta know who was left at camp an' I hada tell him, Oh God, how I hated ta tell him, but I couldn't lie ta him. I told him I didn't know how, but we was gonna git him outta there. That's when he told me what I had ta do. He couldn't face bein' hung, his spirit would never rest or make its way to the other place. I must help him. He could not bear the thought of dyin' like a coward an' thief on a white mans scaffold.

"Kill the man I love? How could he ask this of me? Ain't I been through nough with the death of my children an' all the others that I love, now he wanted me ta take his life. No, no, no, I couldn't do that!

"Henry grew quiet. I knew the look on his face even though I couldn't see him. His pride an' honor was so important to him as a man that I would have ta help him die the way he wanted.

"Sobbin', I asked him how I could help him without hurtin him too much. He jist chuckled at my foolishness; kill him without hurtin' him, how silly.

" 'My mother, Morning Star, has a root that will make me sleep till I reach the other side. I need that root to help me to face the choice I'm makein.'

"My beautiful Henry sleepin' was somethin' I always like ta watch. Many a night I sat by his side watchin' him sleep an' thankin' the stars he was mine.

"I hurried back ta what was left of the camp an' found Morning Star holdin' Small Horse an' rockin'.

"When she heard what I needed an' why, she searched till she found her medicine bag, diggin' deep she come up with a strange lookin' root, handin it ta me she went back ta rockin' the child.

"I was gettin' so tired, I wasn't sure I could make it back ta town one more time an' yet I had ta. I couldn't fail Henry in the only thing he ever asked me ta do.

"It was startin' ta break day when I got back ta the jail, I tossed the root at the barred window but it hit agin a bar an' bounced back. Henry whispered, 'Try agin an' hurry, the sheriff is startin' ta stir round.' The next time the root went through the openin' an' I listened and then I heard Henry sigh. I whispered 'Goodbye my love.' He never answered.

"I set there on the ground I didn't care if they caught me or not. I was too tired ta move an' everythin' I had ta live fer was gone. My world ended with my man.

"When the sheriff went ta wake Henry, I heard him shakin' an' cursin' bout beatin' the townsfolk out of their lynchin' party. A small boy saw me an' went runnin' ta the sheriff shoutin' bout the crazy lady settin' on the ground an' cryin'. When he come round an' saw me, he knew I give Henry the way ta beat the rope.

" 'Well, injun lover, are ya happy now? Ya ain't got a white family an' we took care of that pack of injuns ya was livin' with, so now yer alone just the way ya should be.'

"I didn't waste time answerin' him. It wouldn't do no good.

"I picked myself up an' walked away from a man that had no soul.

"Back at the camp I busied myself fixin' Morning Star's wound, took her an' the child inta the woods in case the men from town come back ta finish the job.

"They'd wiped out the whole tribe cept fer two women an' a boy. Small Horse was the onlyest one of our tribe that was left ta carry on the traditions. Morning Star give me the torn paper that said we owned the land by the bay. I tucked it way with the marriage paper that the preacher give me when he married me an' Henry.

"Not much ta show for all those years, but I didn't much care now that my sons an Henry was gone."

The tears were streaming down my face when she told me her secret. How many women could see her children murdered, help her husband to die an honorable death and still go on all these years?

"When Morning Star had rested we told the child ta hide in the trees till we got back an' we went inta town ta git Henry's body, but they wouldn't let us have it. The sheriff said, 'He's scheduled ta be hung an' that's what he's gonna be.' Can ya believe it? They hung his poor lifeless body on the gallows. It didn't count no how, Henry's spirit was already safe on the other side.

"Just then the army rode in an' the captain asked what was goin' on here, the sheriff told him that they just hung a injun fer rustlin'.

"That captain laughed an' laughed, 'Ya hung a dead man? Looks like he was a whole lot smarter then you! You couldn't kill his spirit.'

"He turn ta me an asked, 'Madam, are you here for this man's body?' I jist nodded. 'Sargent, cut down that man and put him on a horse for these ladies, they want to bury there dead.'

"Takin' the reins, we led the horse an' it's lifeless burden away from those upstandin' Christians."

"Morning Star called the boy from his hidin' place an' let him watch while we got Henry ready fer burial. He needed ta know all these things an' he was the last one left ta pass on the traditions ta his children.

"We buried Henry an' the others in the patch of ground that was made sacred many, many years ago. The spirits could join their ancestors in the other place, not wander the earth. All the tribe is buried there, cept me an' I want ta be buried there, too, right long side my Henry an' the boys. Did I tell ya we buried the boys' tagether so they wouldn't be fraid when they went ta the other side?

"I want ya ta look at the papers that I kept safe fer all these years an' ya can tell me if I owe anybody anythin' fer that there hospital room."

She took the two folded pieces of paper from the medicine bag she wore on a string around her neck, and handed them to me. The paper was stained brown from the years and was permanently creased; the documents were very fragile but, still legible. I was holding a piece of history in my hands. I carefully unfolded the precious papers.

It was a deed to sixteen hundred and forty acres right here in the middle of town.

The land had been deeded to Gray Fox's grandfather, Ravens Wing, for rescuing Griswold's niece from a small band of Sanks, a warlike and powerful tribe occupying the Saginaw Valley. It was signed by the Secretary of the Michigan Territory, the Honorable Stanley Griswold, and was stamped with his official seal, in the year eighteen hundred and six.

These people who lived and farmed in this town were trespassing on the land of the Ojibway! They had stolen the land from the tribe they hated. The very same people who looked down on and punished the Indians for stealing their cattle had done even worse. They had killed a whole tribe of good and gentle people.

"Mina! As sole survivor of the tribe, I believe you own the whole town!"

"Yup, kin ya belive that, first they stole it then they give it back, then they stole it again.

"Don't want the whole town, jist my patch out there where my family is buried. Sides white folk' cain't ever really own lands of the Indian. I may have turned Indian in the eyes of the folks in town, but my blood is not Ojibway.

"Morning Star lasted a coupla days on the trail ta the big falls, then she fell over an' her spirit went home. Me an' Small Horse hada turn back ta bury her with Gray Wolf. I put her on the horse the captain give us an' we started back ta the burial grounds. We run inta nother band of Ojibway movin' through the area, headin' north ta the falls. Their chief asked ta adopt Small Horse an' I said 'yes.' He needed a father ta teach him the ways of the people.

"The town folk looked down on us fer livin' close ta nature. "When we hide an' stalk our enemies they call us cowards an' treacherous, but it was the way the braves was showed how ta survive. It let the brave win over his enemy without harmin' hisself. Cain't stalk the enemy or game if ya march right out in the open. They never did try understandin' indian ways!"

"After buryin' Morning Star I made up my mind those folks ain't gonna run me off. I had ever right ta be here an' care fer my loved ones. I built a lean-to ta stash my few belongin's in; an' headed inta town ta find some kinda work.

"The minister's wife hired me on the spot; said 'everbody should be fergiven one mistake.' I didn't think lovin' Henry was a mistake, but I didn't tell her that.

"She was a bothersome woman, always rubbin' her finger over her furniture ta see if I remembered ta dust, sniffin' the room when she walked in ta see if I been smokin' in the house.

"The minister was a little man with big fat cheeks that looked like he was smilin' all the time.

"His gray hair made a ring round the shiny top that must have bothered him cause he was always pettin' it. I useta think ta myself how these two ever got tagather. She bein' so big and noisy, an' him bein' so small an' quiet. The thought of those two bein' in bed tagather gave me more then a few chuckles. They did treat me fair an' a whole lot bettern the rest of the folks. The others looked at me like I was lowern one of the dogs that ran loose in the town.

"When I had nough money ta build my place, I left. I could fish fer food; trap fer skins and plant corn ta make meal. I needed my time ta spend takin' care of the sacred ground. That's all I needed ta keep me strong."

It had grown dark while she talked, but I wasn't about to stop her now. We had grown so close over these past few months that I couldn't bear to leave her like this. I had my story and the reasons behind Mina's dedication to her task. I wondered if she ever blamed herself for Henry's death, but that is one question I would never ask.

68

Chapter Five

"I still remember the camp by the falls where we was so happy. The warm soft winds on a summer night, the sounds of children playin' by the campfire, an' most of all the gift of bein' safe. When I tell Henry that, he tells me he remembers the touch of my skin, the softness of my hair, an' the fire in my love. Ain't that jist like Henry, always teasin'!"

I refolded the precious papers that Mina had shown me, rose to give them back to her. She shook her head and motioned for me to put them in my purse. She slid down on the lumpy old sofa and drifted off to sleep.

Sitting there watching that brave, wonderful woman who had survived such misery and heartaches, I thought about half the marriages of our time.

Fleeting stabs at security, trial marriages, and trial separations. I came to the conclusion that we all could take a page from Mina's book on faithfulness and loyalty. I resolved to take a closer look at my behavior over the last couple of years and see if there was anything that I could do to rectify my mistakes.

I must have fallen asleep too, but I could have sworn I was awake when Henry came. He was standing next to Mina, holding her hand, inviting her to join him. Her smile lit the room. She looked back at me as they walked into a field of golden grain. I felt the breeze on my face and reaching out to wave goodbye knocked over a box of Mina's papers. The noise made me jump, but she never stirred. Was it a dream that Henry was here? It had to be a dream, as I had never even seen a picture him, yet I knew it was Henry.

From the stories Mina told me, "The People" put great faith in dreams. Was I becoming a believer too? Rubbing my eyes to relieve the grainy feel, I went to the sleeping Mina and touched her hand. There was no life left in that empty body that lay on that broken down resting-place. She had, indeed, taken Henry's hand and followed him to the other side.

There was no rush to summon the police or notify the next of kin. I spent the next few hours reading some of the papers she had saved over the years. She had written little notes on some of the clippings. One read, "This is the obituary of the sheriff, I knowed I'd see him in hell!" Another read, "This is the article bout my mother's death. Never even knew she was sick." One article tells of the shoot out on a Sunday morning when farmer Roth caught two of his tavern cronies cutting up one of his prize bulls.

Mr. Roth seemed to be the victim of rustlers again, but this time he caught them in the act. One of the recent rustlers was the very same person that had seen the Indians killing the Roth's steers the first time. That story made this reporter wonder if the Indians were really responsible the first time. The words in bold print read: **Henry Youngblood always maintained his innocence right to the end. If this speculation were true, then a terrible injustice has been done to the poor red man and we owe them our deepest apology.**

Written in spidery little print are the words: "You owe em more than that!"

Tears blurred my vision. I couldn't go on reading these scraps of a woman's life right now; I needed time to re-examine each fragmentary clue.

I drove back to the farm where I had first reported her collapse and asked if I could use the phone again. When I finally reached someone to report the death of Mina, I was told that they were out to lunch and would be here as soon as they could. The police arrived first then the ambulance. The attendants took one look, wrapped her in a sheet, put her on the gurney and prepared to take her away. Before they covered her completely I asked for the bearskin bag that hung from her neck.

One of the attendants reached in and gently lifting her tiny head, slipped the cord from her person. Handing the precious bag to me he said, "Sure, can't do any harm since you're the only family she's got, and she sure as hell don't have anything of value."

I waited until they all left and taking the bag I sat on down on the chair where my friend and I had shared some memories.

Opening the bag I found a note in her weak scribbly handwriting. She requested that I never tell the towns folk who owns the land. "Tell only the people that need ta know so's we kin have our sacred ground. This kin be our little secret. Here is a list of all the names and where they are restin'. I would like it ta be carved in stone so all will know. No fences round our plot of ground!"

I knew that somewhere in a happier place Mina and her family was enjoying this joke on those greedy, prejudicial white men.

Why Mina chose me to tell her story I can only speculate. Maybe she was facing her own mortality and knew the location of "The People" would be lost forever if she didn't act now. She may have felt it was time for the truth to be told, or maybe it was because I was the only one who had ever asked.

When my attorney and I presented the papers to the governor of the state in a very private meeting, he was only too glad to declare that piece of land an Indian Cemetery and put it on the list for state monies to maintain it.

One year later, I visited Mina's favorite place and found it transformed just as she would have wished.

At the entrance sat a huge stone monument with an eagle clutching a scabbard of arrows. The carver evidently knew the symbol of this tribe. Instead of a totem, they had this monument to identify them forever.

On my first visit to the graves I found that each had a marble stone with the name of the inhabitant etched into it. I checked my list and found that all were recorded and accurate.

At last the people were given the care and respect they deserved. Mina had seen to that.

Would I write my story? No, at least not right away. I would give her descendents time to review their callus treatment of a woman who was so filled with courage. After all, I had given my word to Mina, and she had taught me that dedication and loyalty are worth more to the human spirit than the feeble acclaim that one might receive from this world.

When the dust had settled, I called Jim and invited him out for a visit. After a dinner of all his favorite foods, we sat talking over coffee. I told him about Mina and the great sacrifices that she had made to keep her husband and children close to her, even in death. When I finished my tale of the heroic little woman with a big heart, he smiled.

"I haven't seen you this excited about anything in a long time. This adventure was just what you needed to bring you back to us. Jamie and I have missed that vibrant, caring, woman you used to be."

I realized then that I was the one that had pulled away and isolated myself from both of them. Mina had taught me to savor all the small pleasures that life gives and value them more than gold. They are gifts from God.

Jim and I are remarried now and we take the time to enjoy each and every moment together. We spend our vacations at the cottage in Michigan.

Jamie sometimes comes up on school breaks, but she is dating Sammy, her best friends brother, so her schedule is quite full. We love seeing her and she and her friends are always welcome, but Jim and I no longer feel we need other people around to be comfortable.

Mina gave me a gift when she taught me the real meaning of love.

Every so often I get lonely for that feisty little lady and visit the cemetery in the woods. Sitting on the ground near Henry and Mina's graves, I listen to the whispering in the pines. I'm enthralled by the wind playfully dancing through the birch trees, creating faint melodious sounds of the flute and conjuring up second hand memories of warm nights, campfires, and low murmurs of love. I'm so grateful for the gift of joy Mina shared with me.

Sometimes I hear the rustle of dry leaves and wonder if Mina's little friend, the field mouse, visits too.

The end

74

Author's notes:

In a perfect world the end of this tale would be true, but sadly it is not. We are just beginning to realize how important it is to preserve the heritage of all people.

We have violated millions upon millions of Native American grave sites in the name of progress, gathered relics from the desecrated holy ground and displayed them in our museums and in our homes. The bones of fathers, mothers, grandfathers, grandmothers, and God help us, the bones of children.

We travel millions of miles to foreign lands to fight for the rights of other nations and we totally close our eyes to the plight of our brothers and sisters, the Native American.

A good friend Sandi Harrington, told me and I quote, "Indians come in all sizes, shapes, and colors. There is no such thing as part Indian, either you are or you aren't, your heart knows."

Search your heart for that drop of Indian that is in you and stand up for fairness and justice. Let's stop destroying the holy burial grounds of our brothers and sisters.

Let them sleep in peace.

Miigwetch, Miigwetch

76

The author.....

Barbara Neveau is a resident of Essexville, Michigan and mother of three grown children. Finding time on her hands at the age of 65, she went back to school for her high school diploma.

While working for her credits she discovered her passion for writing. With the encouragement of her family, friends, and teachers she began writing short stories.

"Cemetery of the Lost" is one of her favorite tales based on facts she gathered while doing a genealogy of her own family.

If you would like to purchase autographed
copies of
Cemetery of the Lost
you may send $12.95 per copy, plus $4.00 shipping and
handling to:

Barbara Neveau
P.O. Box 32
Essexville, MI 48732

If you would like to contact the author you may
contact her at the above address or email her at:
PenScratcher@hotmail.com